P9-DVO-697

BOY SOUP

Written by Loris Lesynski

Illustrated by Michael Martchenko

annick press
Toronto • New York • Vancouver

To "The Goup"

©2008 Loris Lesynski (text)
©2008 Michael Martchenko (art)
©1996 Loris Lesynski (original edition)
Design/Loris Lesynski, *Laugh Lines Design*
Back cover photo: Susan Shipton

Annick Press Ltd.

We acknowledge the support of the Canada Council for the Arts,
the Ontario Arts Council, and the Government of Canada through
the Book Publishing Industry Development Program (BPIDP)
for our publishing activities.

ONTARIO ARTS COUNCIL
CONSEIL DES ARTS DE L'ONTARIO

Cataloging in Publication

Lesynski, Loris
    Boy soup / written by Loris Lesynski ; illustrated by Michael Martchenko.

Originally publ. under title: Boy soup, or, When Giant caught cold.
Target audience: For ages 4-7.
ISBN 978-1-55451-143-3 (bound).—ISBN 978-1-55451-142-6 (pbk.)

    I. Martchenko, Michael II. Title.

    PS8573.E79B69 2008   jC813'.54   C2008-901533-9

    The art in this book was rendered in watercolor.
    The text was typeset in Utopia.

Distributed in Canada by: Published in the U.S.A. by Annick Press (U.S.) Ltd.
    Firefly Books Ltd.   Distributed in the U.S.A. by:
    66 Leek Crescent   Firefly Books (U.S.) Inc.
    Richmond Hill, ON   P.O. Box 1338
    L4B 1H1   Ellicott Station
                                    Buffalo, NY 14205

Printed and bound in China.

                    visit us at: **www.annickpress.com**
                    visit Loris at: **www.lorislesynski.com**

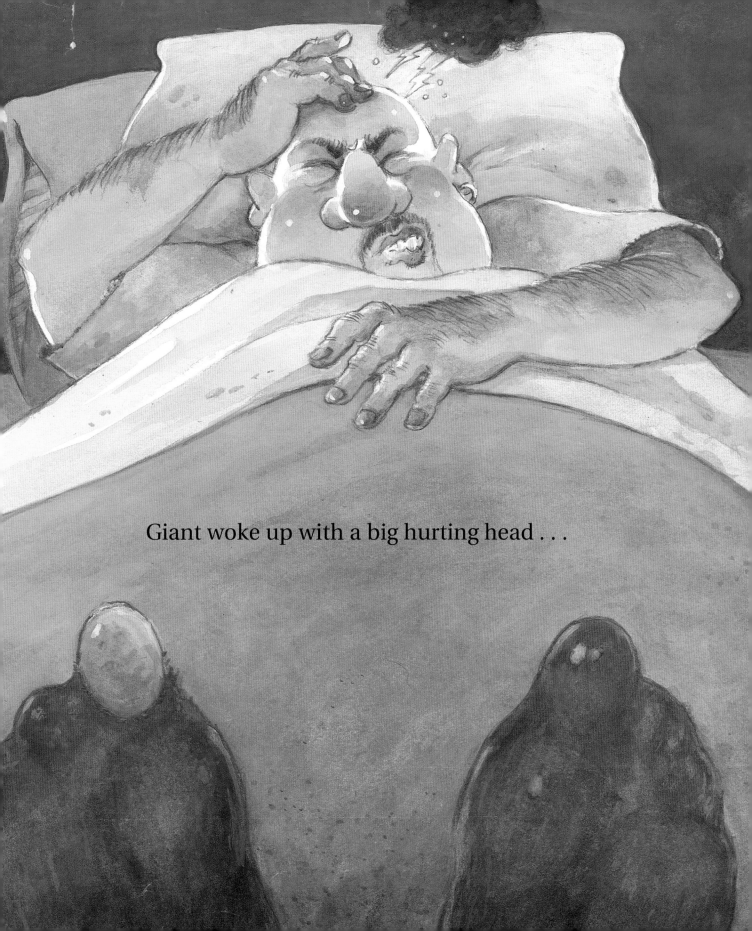

Giant woke up with a big hurting head . . .

"I am sore I am sick I feel awful," he said.

He coughed—
    moving mountains.
He hacked—
    causing quakes.
He said with a whimper,
    "My everything aches."

Groaning, he shoveled his blankets aside
and reached for his *Giants
Home Medical Guide.*

With sofa-sized fingers,
  he leafed through the book,
and in between sneezes
  so loud that he shook,
he found all his symptoms—
  page seventy-one:

"Queasiness,
  wheeziness,
  coughing begun.
  Completely depleted
  and tending to droop."

The only prescription?

"A bowl of
Boy Soup."

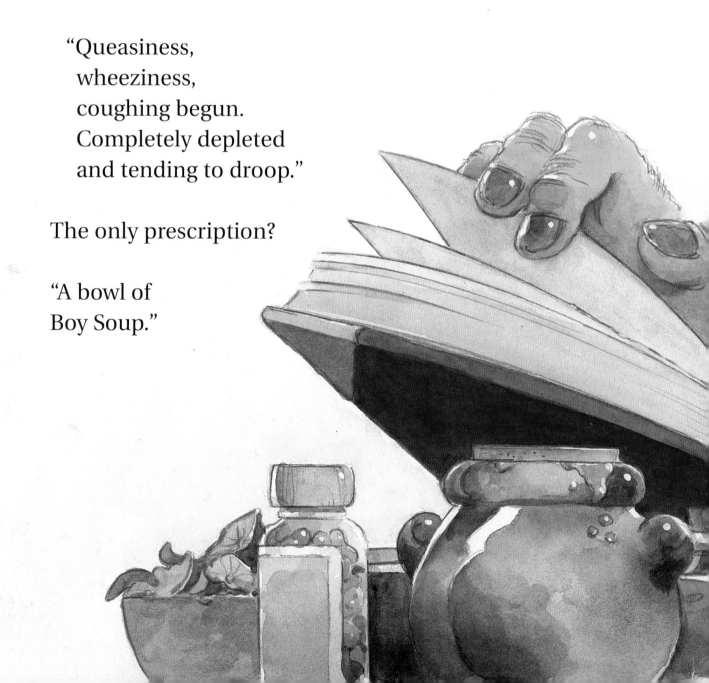

"Can't *be*," said the giant. "Would be a disgrace."
  But a big greedy grin spread all over his face.

"Of course, if I'm ill, that's a decent excuse.
    And think of the broth
       a good boy could produce.
    A sweet boy, a neat boy,
       a boy so delicious
    a giant might find himself
       licking the dishes . . .

One buttery boy—or better, a group.
    A half-dozen lads would make
       wonderful soup!"

Catching the boys was as easy as pie:
  he stretched down his thick giant arm through the sky
and rested his hand at the top of a tree
  where children were playing—they just didn't see
    the branch they were grabbing
        could grab *them.*
              Too late!

That's how the giant got five boys—
and Kate.

"Why *should* I feel guilty?"
the giant began
when six angry children
protested his plan.

"It's here in this authorized
medical book!"

Kate asked, "Before supper,
could *I* have a look?"

She read every word
in the faded ink
and said, "May I have
just a minute to think?"

—but "**NO!**" snapped the giant. "Boys, *into* the pot!
  I've chills and a fever,
    I'm cold and I'm hot."
      And then with a thunderous splat blew his nose
        as the boys shook with fear
          from their heads to their toes.

      Kate racked her brain at a furious rate
        to save all her friends from this hideous fate.

      The giant was ready.

        How could they flee?

Their ten rubber running shoes—
that was the key!

Just as the giant came closer to scoop
   the lads for his horrid medicinal soup,
Kate gave a signal, the tiniest look.
   The boys understood.
They leapt to the book
               and started a dance, half a shuffle, half-run,
                  and jogged back and forth on page seventy-one.
                     Up the page, *down* the page,
                        sidestep, repeat—

—'til most
     of each word
          was erased
               by their feet.

"Now I can't check it!"
the giant complained.
But Kate said, "I've read it,
I'll gladly explain.
The book said quite clearly,
of this I am sure—
Boy Soup is soup *made* by boys,
that's the cure."

"But . . ." sniffed the giant,
"I thought boys went *in* it . . .
I think I'm confused . . .
can you give me a minute?"

"*Oh, no,*" Kate proclaimed. "You're too sick, don't you know.
We have to work fast. Come on, fellows, let's go!"

The boys cooked the carrots ✓
　　the boys boiled the peas ✓
then seasoned the soup
　　with a handful of fleas ✓

They put in
　　some mud ✓
　　some thick yellow glue ✓
　　and a generous dollop of dandruff shampoo ✓

Kate poured in
　　pepper ✓
　　red hot sauce ✓
　　really, really, really, *really* rotten bananas ✓
　　and candy floss ✓
　　sour green pickles ✓
　　and beans in the can ✓
—all simmered together
　　　as part of the plan.

And oh, the aroma!
　　Like skunk in a pot.

　　　　Kate smiled her sweetest
　　　　　and served it up hot.

In between snuffles, the giant took sips
        from a spoon trembling close
            to his great hairy lips.

He scowled in suspicion but took one more taste
    with a huge doughy tongue much the color of paste—

then tipped the whole potful of soup down his throat
        . . . sat back
            . . . and *sighed*
                —'til he started to bloat!

And the pepper, the mud, and the pickles
            combined.

The giant let out a most terrible whine—

—and SPIT out the soup
  with so mighty a blast
that it blew
  all the children
down homeward at last.

Kate and the fellows
    were dented, but sound,
when they landed back
    home on familiar ground . . .

They needed new sneakers,
and something to do
to get over the horrible shock
they'd been through.

The *giant* was not
who they wanted to feed.
But they *had* liked the cooking,
with Kate in the lead.

So they opened Boys' Restaurant
as a group
—and served almost everything
but Boy Soup.

One day at the diner, delivery came
of an extra-large envelope bearing Kate's name.

The giant had written:

I *did* get your letter.

Thank you for asking,

I *am* feeling better.

That Medical Book is from long, long ago.
They boiled little boys then,
even though
you're *RIGHT* that it's wrong—
I guess that I knew it—
but feeling so sick made me tempted
to do it.
I'm *glad* that you tricked me.
I would have felt bad
when later I realized
I'd eaten a lad.

I told all the giants:
no Boy Soup for me!

Sorry again.
Yours sincerely,
Big G.